GET OFF MY LAWN!

Anna Ceguerra

Published by A Whim Away PTY LTD

a-whim-away.com

Cover artwork, cover credit: Marta Khmilyar.

Author portrait credit: The University of Sydney / Louise Cooper.

NATIONAL LIBRARY OF AUSTRALIA

A catalogue record for this book is available from the National Library of Australia

This book is available in print, audio and ebook formats.

ISBN-10 (print): 0-6454823-0-7
ISBN-13 (print): 978-0-6454823-0-0

To Lola Gloria.

Acknowledgements

In self-publishing, ultimately the book is under my name, but I'll tell you a secret: many hands made light work.

I want to thank Adam Guetti and Ed Pugh, for their kind words and generosity during our writing mentoring sessions.

To the writing groups I have been part of. First, the Inner West Write Club, hosted by Marrickville Library and Meetup, and led by Oula, Gazala, Maree and Maria, thank you for providing a platform for my work. Second, the writing group in St John of God led by Jonathan, thank you for the encouragement and for starting me off on this journey.

To Katie Yee, for the developmental edit, and letting me see that the changes needed weren't so extensive after all.

To Pam Sewell, for the accurate copyedit and proofread.

To Bronwyn Mehan, Marty Gallagher, and Lewis Scamozzi from Spineless Wonders, for the audiobook.

To Marta Khmilyar, for the cover illustration and cover design.

To the Self Publishing Support Group on Facebook,

for help with all things self-publishing.

To Minuteman Press Banksmeadow, for printing my book copies in Sydney, Australia.

To the readers of my first novella, Cupid's Kiss. Thank you for the wonderful support, I hope you enjoy this different story just as equally.

I acknowledge the support of the Australian Government. Thank you for providing excellent programs such as the NDIS, NEIS and Medicare. In particular I would like to mention Tam, Sophie, Helen, Louise, Hisayo, Matthew, Adam, Nick, Eleni, Sam x2, Martina, Orian, Noel, Anna, Kate, and Philip, who have helped me recently through these programs.

To my closest friends, Lisa, Billie, Belinda, Katie, thank you for all the hijinx, both on-line and off-.

To my family, R, C, and P, thank you for being there for me.

I would also like to mention the dearly departed: Mum, and Lola Gloria. Lola, this book is for you.

CHAPTER ONE

August

Olivia opened her eyes. She was still here. She lay in her bed for another minute, squandering the seconds. "I hate Mondays," she thought. The idea was reflexive, despite Olivia's long retirement from her tech dev job. Monday was the same as any other day.

It was so early, not even the birds had awakened from their slumber. The sky held a promising tinge of light while waiting for the dawn. Peaceful times like this filled Olivia with anxiety, even though her days followed a well-worn routine. She stretched in bed, clicking stiff joints and loosening muscles from an adequate night of sleep before easing herself towards the edge of the bed to begin her daily exercises.

First, she balanced on one foot before swapping to the other. Then dumbbells made an appearance. Finally, she used the Theraband for resistance training. The balance and strength exercises had maintained her movement as she aged to avoid serious falls. So Olivia was now an active and healthy ninety-year-old, still able to live on her own, albeit with a little help.

She was mostly content this way. Olivia had lived her life to the fullest and was ready for the end. Whenever that may be.

CHAPTER TWO

New Neighbours

Later that day, the old woman straightened her back, and looked up and across her pristine lawn—not a blade of grass out of place. Passers-by on her quiet street often complimented her efforts as she watered, fertilised, or cut it to perfection. Before, she thought of it as her husband's pride and joy, but it was now hers to care for. Just like the rest of the house. All to herself.

All of her children had moved far away long ago, although she did get the occasional visit from their families. Each child had built homes and lives of their own now. She was the only one left here. To avoid arguments later, each had claimed what they wanted in the house, and Olivia listed the items in a small ledger. She liked to believe the things she owned were still wanted.

A car cruised up to the house next door, which had sold

three months ago. The front lawn had turned brown over the winter, with nobody to care for it. A group of four piled out: two similar men and two young children. The eldest seemed around ten years old, the youngest probably seven. One man lifted the little one onto his hip, and she snuggled into the awkward-looking embrace. The driver of the vehicle saw Olivia and waved cheerfully. Olivia offered a hesitant wave in return.

"Hi, I'm James," he said in a measured but friendly tone, approaching her to offer his hand.

Olivia waved him away. "Sorry, dear, my hands are filthy from gardening. I'm Olivia."

James dropped the hand back by his side, smile wavering, but he powered on. "Hi, Olivia. That's my partner, Luke, and our two daughters. I won't bombard you with their names."

This surprised Olivia. She judged by their round faces, tall, slight bodies and black hair that they were brothers. Yet she waved at them and raised her voice until it faltered. "Hello!"

"Honey, we're just going to open up the house before the truck comes," Luke boomed in a deep voice over his shoulder, as the two children ran ahead, squealing excitedly. After Luke led the children into the house,

Olivia heard them open the windows from inside. Outside, there was only an awkward silence.

"Well, I'd better go help them," said James, and he walked towards his new home.

CHAPTER THREE

September

Her. Pristine. Lawn. Olivia trudged from her garage, carrying an electric whipper snipper. The job took time, but she had to straighten the edge of her beautiful lawn. The beauty of buffalo grass meant it didn't need much maintenance—it stayed short all year.

As she worked her way around the entire front garden, she noticed the two girls running about on the brown lawn next door, feet crunching on the dead grass. Olivia shook her head as she remembered her softly spoken neighbour trying to revive the lawn a few days back, but it was too far gone. They would need to lay new turf.

"Girls, time to eat!" the other man called loudly from inside the house. They both ran in as Olivia watched.

Her own kids didn't play on their lawn while they were

growing up. It all started when her husband, Adam, bought a cubby house and placed it on the lawn. A few weeks later, when he moved it to another spot, the blades of grass had turned yellow underneath. Adam was furious at himself for not realising. From that day forward, he forbade their girls to play on the front lawn, and the cubby house disappeared forever.

Olivia caught a glint of bright red on the far edge of the lawn. She turned off the whipper snipper and bent to inspect the object. It was a toy car. She gathered it up, the metal cold against her palm. Olivia scanned the street, but saw no-one, so she dropped the toy into her pocket, and returned to the task.

CHAPTER FOUR

Chit Chat

A week later, it was time to tend to the lawn again. As Olivia brought the whipper snipper around the corner of her house, she saw the flurry of a small, black animal streak past. Olivia squinted as she tried to figure out her nemesis' lair, with a fleeting irritation.

She didn't have many enemies, but Olivia had found one in this scrawny black cat. For the past month, the stray kept leaving its scat all over her lawn, and she couldn't figure out how to get rid of him. The poop left a foul smell, likely because of the cat's poor diet, and Olivia could barely go near it to pick it up and throw it away.

As she scanned the street, she saw one of her male neighbours standing on his lawn, looking dejected. Olivia called out her guess at one of their names and they exchanged pleasantries.

"Are you thinking of re-turfing?" Olivia asked.

James cast a longing gaze over her lawn and heaved a sigh. "Yes, thinking is as far as I'll get... Your lawn is beautiful, by the way. It was the first thing I noticed when we moved in."

"Thank you, dear. My late husband researched it, laid it himself and maintained it. He didn't have much that he called his own except the lawn, so I keep it neat and tidy for him now."

"Oh, that's lovely." He looked at her. "Can I ask, how long ago did your husband pass away?"

"About twenty years ago now," said Olivia. James shot her a sympathetic smile, lost for words. But Olivia didn't want sympathy. "I expected to die of a broken heart, but alas, that did not happen."

He looked down. "I know how you feel... The girls' mother left me a couple of years ago. We're still going through the divorce and—"

"I'm sorry to hear that, dear," Olivia interrupted, and put her safety goggles on. "Anyway, I'd better get on with it. Nice talking with you."

James gaped like a stunned goldfish for a moment

before stuttering. "Y-you too, Olivia."

CHAPTER FIVE
Painting

Olivia sat in her front room. Her window was open on this still spring morning, ready for the breeze when it eventually chose to stir. For some reason, she dreamt of her husband wearing red last night.

She mentally blocked out all distractions as she started mixing different varieties of red, adding a bit of yellow to this or blue to that, or both. When she felt satisfied, she turned with her palette towards the easel. Olivia dabbed bits of the paint onto the canvas, slowly building up the field of flowers in her mind.

From the corner of her eye, a red hat bounced past her window, singing a nursery rhyme in time with each scuff of a shoe. Olivia frowned and moved towards the commotion. It was the little girl from next door.

"Hey!" Olivia shouted as much as her voice would

allow.

The girl, clearly within earshot, stood still when she heard the call, then scurried out of eyesight.

Distraction sorted, Olivia tried to return to her painting. She looked at the canvas from a different angle and sighed. What she had pictured to be a calming field of scarlet flowers, more closely resembled a devastated field spotted with blood. She would have to start again. Maybe tomorrow.

CHAPTER SIX

Meet Cute

Despite the butterflies in her stomach, Olivia stood on the ladder in front of her house, fitting a 360-degree view camera onto the ceiling of her patio. She finished drilling the last screw in and stepped down from the ladder.

Across her lawn, the youngest girl stood in her new driveway, watching on. Frozen to the spot, the silent child disturbed Olivia.

"Oh! Hello dear, I didn't see you there. I'm Olivia. What's your name?" The girl mumbled something, and Olivia cupped a hand against her ear. "What was that, dear? I can't hear you."

"DOTTY!" She screamed, and ran inside her house.

Olivia gasped and fell backwards, almost tripping on

the ladder. Her heart raced for a moment while she leaned against the railing. As she regained her composure, one of Dotty's fathers appeared with the girl hiding behind him.

"Go on, Dotty," he said to her reassuringly.

"Hi, Mrs. Olivia. My name is Dotty and I'm seven years old," she clearly enunciated each syllable.

"Nice to meet you, Dotty. My goodness, you gave me a fright back there!" Olivia rested her hand on the ladder. "Thank you... Luke?"

"Yeah, sorry about that. She's still learning how to introduce herself," Luke admitted in his outside voice. "She hasn't met many new people."

"I see," Olivia said, relieved that she could tell the difference between the two men now. When they were together, it was easy. It was when they were apart that it was a challenge.

Dotty looked at Luke, almost defiantly, grabbing the fabric of his jeans.

"It's okay, dear..." Olivia didn't quite know what to say next. *What type of childhood had Dotty experienced to rarely meet new people?* "You know, I noticed someone with a red hat run past my front window the other day. Would you know who it was?"

Dotty's hands sprang to the top of head, where her red hat still sat. She slowly shook her head.

"Well, if you see them, please tell them to stay off my lawn. It's very important. Can you do that for me?"

Dotty put her arms down and hugged Luke's legs again, shaking her head and burying it into Luke's thigh.

Olivia sighed dramatically. "If they don't keep off the lawn, I guess there's no way for me to keep an eye on the cat, then."

Dotty peeked past Luke's jeans. "... Cat?"

"Yes dear, there's a cat that keeps pooping on the lawn. I'm trying to catch it in the act, but I haven't been able to yet." Olivia pointed at the camera. "That's why I installed that, so the motion detectors can capture when it happens."

"Why don't you want the cat to poop on your lawn?" Dotty had given up the pretence of hiding.

"Well, it's smelly, messy, and my lawn needs to be perfect for when the time comes."

Dotty's brow furrowed as she considered Olivia's

words. "Perfect? For when the time comes?"

"That's right, dear. For when the time comes."

CHAPTER SEVEN

Snip

Snip. Snip.

It was in her dreams again. The sound scissors make during a haircut. Olivia startled awake around midnight and found herself too anxious to sleep. She tried her deep breathing and self-soothing exercises, but it was no use. She returned to her bed for the fifth time and shut her eyes.

Snip. Snip.

Once again, Olivia jolted up in her bed and she glanced at the clock. She was relieved to discover it was almost her regular wake-up time. Still, the broken sleep had tired Olivia and left her eyes scratchy, so her motions were distracted as she moved through her dawn ritual.

After completing the routine, Olivia's head had cleared

enough for her to remember the camera. The new device contained a motion sensor, but also kept a record of the ten seconds before the event happened. There were many recordings, most capturing cars or passers-by, and Olivia flicked through them with a huff. Not one showed the damn cat.

Then she saw something unexpected. A child appearing to squat on the edge of her lawn, an hour after sunset. The resolution of the image didn't provide enough detail. They were crouching for at least a minute, then left. Olivia searched the week's worth of recordings, and each time, the child arrived like clockwork. She wondered what they could be doing and started to formulate a plan.

CHAPTER EIGHT

First Attempt

Later that evening, Olivia sat alert in the gathering darkness in her front room. In front of her lay a new device she bought, designed to emit a high-pitched noise. It was mainly used to repel mosquitos, but from the specifications, she had a theory that it would also affect children.

When Olivia opened the packaging earlier, she'd pursed her lips in concentration, wondering how well it would work. She loved new gadgets. For now, she put it aside to concentrate on the lawn before her.

The street lamp illuminated two children this time, surprising Olivia. The kids next door. She waited until they found their chosen position on her lawn, the pair crouching low.

Snip. Snip.

The children's heads were down close to the ground, trying to see what they were doing despite the dusky light. Then it dawned on her. The children were cutting her lawn! Outrage boiled inside her like a threatening storm. She was so incensed she almost forgot the device in front of her.

She tapped the red button. A faint red light blinked on when it was pressed, but otherwise nothing happened. She looked outside the window, and the children were still snipping away. Olivia pressed the button for longer. Still nothing.

Olivia swore and released the button, and the eldest waved her hand around as if she was swatting a mosquito. Curious, she tried pressing the button for a shorter period. Again, when Olivia released it, the big sister waved a wild hand in the air. Dotty, however, remained unaffected.

The girls ran off and left Olivia with her failed attempts, and the realisation she'd need more than just a small device.

CHAPTER NINE

Gadgets

As the week progressed, the kids didn't stay in one spot. Instead, they moved to a different section every night, and Olivia couldn't capture their vandalism. Even her inspection of the lawn in the bright daylight the following day failed to provide more answers.

One morning, less than a week later, a large box arrived on Olivia's doorstep. She lifted it easily, then took it into her house. One by one, she unpacked the contents of the almost empty box, which were all covered in bubble wrap.

1 x camera with night vision mode, microphone, and motion sensor, for picking up video, audio and to detect motion.

1 x pair of small outdoor speakers, to project sound

outside.

1 x pair of night vision binoculars, to see things in low light.

1 x stick computer, for processing the camera data.

1 x router, for connecting the camera and speakers with the stick computer.

1 x outdoor casing to protect the camera and speakers from the elements.

There could be an easier way, but the thought was fleeting. Olivia was happy with the new gadgets and the new project. She was a typical tech person who thought of tech solutions before more conventional ones. That's how she'd excelled in her job developing software for the internet of things—IoT—back in the day. Since she and her husband retired, they tried to leave it behind, but once a techie, always a techie.

Olivia swiftly put everything together and installed the software on the stick computer. She would have to wait until evening to test the night vision.

CHAPTER TEN

Snip2

Olivia set up a chair beside the window of her front room—night goggles ready on the windowsill. She connected her laptop with the new stick computer, ready for the incoming images. The sun was still setting, so Olivia needed to be patient a little longer.

While Olivia waited, she recalled her early career successes. In the 2030s, the key growth area was in energy density for batteries. While the energy industry boomed, so did self-powered ultra-miniaturised devices. Her work in connecting these SPUDs to the internet was key to integrating the physical and digital worlds. Yet with all the developments in hardware and software in the past sixty years, she still liked getting her hands dirty.

The computer pinged. Olivia's heart skipped a beat. She looked at the screen as that dratted black cat slunk low, about to pounce. "Lucky the ping didn't happen later," she thought as she ignored the cat and muted her computer. There were more important things to worry about. She looked at the resolution of the glowing green night-vision image on the screen. It was better, but still grainy.

Having been seated for so long, Olivia shuffled away to find a snack in the kitchen while she waited for dark. She chose one of the pre-packaged lasagnes stored in her freezer. The microwave hummed in the otherwise silent house while she waited. She missed the noise of people, children, and dogs in the house. But the thought of people imposing into her space was too infuriating for her now. Three beeps from the microwaves sounded, and she took the hot container to the table, sat, and devoured the heated food alone.

After she put the container into the dishwasher, Olivia snuffed the lights one by one. Instead of going to bed, she sat at the window, hidden by shadows. As expected, the two children came onto her lawn, whispering to each other. Olivia would have to enhance the sound later. They crouched down on different parts of the grass and started snipping. Olivia checked the camera for the blinking red light, then raised the binoculars to her eyes.

Both children were snipping very close to the ground. Olivia's outrage bubbled back to the surface, but she controlled it in time to avoid responding. After fifteen minutes, one child stood, and the other followed, both returning to their house.

CHAPTER ELEVEN
Training

Olivia worked on her computer with the audio and video files she'd captured the previous night. She needed to train the computer to recognise the sound of snipping so it could perform a pre-defined action.

First, she meticulously isolated the snipping sound from the audio last night. Olivia then converted the audio file into data the computer would understand, which she then used to train a neural network. The output was finally associated with her voice but raised several octaves to the higher, inaudible frequencies. She only had fifteen minutes' worth of them snipping, but hoped it was enough.

Before long, her efforts had taken up the whole day. She'd even forgotten about her afternoon gardening. Now a little weary, Olivia took a quick nap before dinner.

When she woke, the room was dark, and she sat up with a start. Had she missed it? Olivia hurried into the front room and checked the camera recording. Having indeed slept through the action, she double-clicked the file and watched the captured video in the dark.

The two kids came, as expected, and started snipping at her lawn. Her audio mixer showed that her high-pitched audio file played after the first snip of a series of cuts. The eldest stopped snipping each time to raise her head, eyes narrowed and nose crinkled. After a few brief moments, she continued snipping. Eventually she stopped altogether, earlier than usual, and said, "Let's go, Dotty, we shouldn't be here."

"In a minute, Susy," Dotty replied.

"Okay, but I'm going now," Susy replied in such a soft whisper that Olivia had to compensate with the software to hear it. Susy glanced at the front window with suspicion and disappeared into her house. About five minutes later, Dotty stopped and followed suit.

Olivia smiled—the high-pitched audio file of her voice repeating "Get off my lawn" had worked…

The next evening, Susy didn't come back. With one child sorted, Olivia now had to work on stopping

Dotty's visits. Olivia tried a few things, but the persistent little girl returned. Olivia would have to go full Pavlov.

Stumped, Olivia tried a variety of inaudible sounds to find something, anything, that Dotty would respond to. Out of pure frustration, she hooked up a song with a strong bass beat, the audible parts removed, and Dotty snipped in time with the tune. Finally, a result. Olivia searched her music library for songs with strong beats and extracted the audible range.

Over the following week, Olivia tested the playlist the moment the snipping started, and stopped as soon as Dotty called it quits. With a pattern in place, Olivia shortened the playlist by one minute, pleased when Dotty stopped, too. Night by night, Olivia shortened the soundtrack until it didn't play at all. Later, Dotty stood on the lawn like a deer caught in headlights but headed home without a single snip.

"That's right, get off my lawn," Olivia whispered under her breath.

CHAPTER TWELVE

Halloween

It was two days before Halloween.

In Australia, children only trick or treat at decorated houses, which Olivia hadn't bothered with in ages. Her late husband had loved the event despite the ruined lawn saga, but she played along with it all. Adam would decorate his perfect front lawn with an abundance of Halloween decorations. One year, he had a blow-up Santa with reindeer, and he dressed Santa like a witch. "It's a way to save with decorations," he had laughed with glee.

With her husband still in her thoughts, Olivia retrieved the whipper snipper and brought it outside. She switched it on and walked around the edges. Not a stray blade of grass in sight. Olivia turned off the unused power tool and stood in disbelief, staring at her already perfectly manicured lawn. She sighed—perhaps the children did a good deed after all.

A tinge of guilt seeded within her, and Olivia hoped to make amends. The next day, she bought the required ingredients to bake a cake, which she also hadn't done in years. She cooked it that morning, then waited until they arrived home from school so she could deliver it in person.

When she knocked on the door, Luke answered, and Olivia held out the bulky cylindrical container. "Hi, Luke, I just thought I'd do the neighbourly thing and make you and the girls a cake for afternoon tea."

"Oh thanks, Olivia. Would you like to join us?" Luke asked. The girls shouted in the background, running down the hallway. When they saw Olivia through the open door, they stopped squealing and skidded to a halt, right into Luke's legs. His knees buckled but did not fall.

"Thank you, dear, but I have things to do," said Olivia, edging away from the door. "Please return the Tupperware when you're finished. It keeps the cake quite fresh."

"Thanks Olivia, will do." Luke took the container and closed her out, but she heard another squeal and excited chatter.

"What is it, Papa?"

CHAPTER THIRTEEN

Decorations

Two nights later, with her conscience clear, Olivia enjoyed a beautiful night's sleep. When she stretched, joints clicking, the following morning, she didn't feel too bothered by it. She didn't feel bothered by anything in particular. She worked through her routine in the morning and was having her mid-afternoon snack when her doorbell rang.

"Trick or treat!" A group of young children with their parents stood ready at the door.

Olivia was confused. "Oh, hello, I wasn't expecting you. I didn't think my lawn was decorated."

"It is, actually," said the frowning mother.

"I don't have anything prepared, I'm afraid."

"That's okay," she said, looking hassled. As the family walked up the driveway, the children screamed, demanding their sweets.

Olivia returned to her front room and opened the window. At first glance, her lawn looked perfect as always, but when the sun shone through the clouds, silver threads shimmered in the light. Curious, Olivia left the house to inspect her front yard. Hand-drawn images of pumpkins, black cats, and other traditional Halloween images were messily stuck on her front fence. The picture of the black cat in particular triggered her momentarily.

Olivia looked in disbelief. *Do they know what they're doing? Do they want lollies from me?* A dozen questions roiled in her mind, each one making her angrier than the last. She thought of her husband decorating the lawn himself, one of the few jobs he enjoyed throughout the year. That was the final straw. *Who do they think they are, trying to replace him?*

She reached out to rip off the closest decoration, but snatched her hand away. A better idea flourished, and Olivia retreated to prepare herself for battle.

CHAPTER FOURTEEN

Revenge

"Trick or treat," came the familiar cry at Olivia's door that evening. This time, however, she was prepared with some scrumptious-looking toffee kiwi fruit slivers, each skewered on bamboo sticks. She opened the door to a group of older children who should be studying rather than knocking on doors.

"Oh, come and take a toffee kiwi fruit, dears," Olivia said with a welcoming smile. She showed them the neat row of sweets assembled in a rectangular plastic container. They took one look at it and grimaced.

"Err, no thanks," they said one by one, and slowly left. In the distance, one of them said, "Yuck, it's fruit!"

Olivia shut the door and giggled like a youngster.

Throughout the evening, waves of trick-or-treaters rang

Olivia's doorbell, and each one turned up their nose at the treat before they left. Between visits, Olivia cackled behind the door. The trick wasn't getting old.

Finally, Susy and Dotty appeared at the door.

"Trick or treat!" they said in loud, sing-song voices as Olivia opened her door.

"Well, if it isn't the two trouble-makers. Did you two put up the decorations on my lawn?"

Susy shook her head as Dotty said, "Yes!" Susy elbowed her younger sister. "I mean, no," she quickly corrected.

"Well, whoever did will get an extra special surprise. Here, girls, take some sweets," Olivia said.

"Thanks, Mrs Olivia," they said in unison as they each took a piece and left, singing a Halloween song.

Olivia closed the door behind them, not cackling this time. She thought she had the perfect fruity revenge, but it seemed the girls were unaffected by her intent.

CHAPTER FIFTEEN

November

The following morning, Olivia had her kitchen window open to let the breeze in. She had just finished her coffee when a girl screamed, "Papa!" Heavy footsteps thudded before the murmur of a male voice and a child's whiny cry drifted from next door.

Five minutes later, she heard the doorbell.

"Olivia—thank goodness you're here. Susy's had an allergic reaction... I think she's eaten something. Could you look after Dotty for me?" Luke asked, raking a hand through his hair. An ambulance pulled into his drive, and Luke stuttered. Holding his hand was Dotty, who carried a toy truck in the crook of her arm.

"I—yes, of course—" Olivia started.

That was enough for Luke. He crouched down to

Dotty's eye level. "Be good for Mrs Olivia. Daddy will be back soon." He kissed her on top of her head and ran back to his house.

A thousand thoughts flew through Olivia's head, but none of them formed a coherent sentence. Underlying these thoughts was the kernel of guilt germinating in her belly. *Did she do this?* Dotty stilled as she entered the house, only her head moving as she took in the alien surroundings.

"Have you eaten breakfast?" Olivia blurted out, anything to break the awkward silence of the past minute. Dotty slowly shook her head. "Okay, let's go into the kitchen."

Olivia led her through the musty hallway, the space filled with overflowing bookshelves from floor to ceiling. When Olivia checked on her charge, she found a look of wonderment on Dotty's face.

"What do you usually have for breakfast?" Olivia asked, breaking the spell.

Dotty quickened her steps to join Olivia and climbed onto a chair. "Papa makes us something different every day."

"Like what?"

Dotty settled into her seat. "Yesterday, we had orange pancakes with swimming spiders on them."

"Orange pancakes? And the day before that?"

"We had Mickey and Minnie pancakes."

"Okay... what else?" Olivia asked.

"Dinosaur pancakes."

Olivia laughed, stopping abruptly when the girl shrank into the seat. "What's your favourite food?"

"Pancakes..." Dotty continued to fiddle with her toy truck.

"Would you like some pancakes now, dear?" Olivia said, her tone serious, but her lips twitched.

"Yes..." the young girl said to her truck, and Olivia got to work.

"That's a nice truck," she mentioned off-hand.

Dotty authoritatively put her truck on the table. "It's a CM-1000 cement mixer, capable of rotating one rev per minute," Dotty rattled off the specs as she pointed to different parts of the truck. Olivia nodded impatiently along the way. Nerds always irked her with their endless recitation of specs. She identified more with the creativity of being a techie.

Dotty continued her tireless spiel, so Olivia interrupted. "Oh, very nice. I don't know much about trucks myself, but I know a fair bit about gadgets and read a lot of books."

"I only have baby books at home."

Olivia expertly flipped the pancake on the frying pan. "We can look at my library later if you want."

Dotty eyes glimmered, but remained glued to her truck, so Olivia let her be while she finished cooking the pancake. When she served the plain circle on a plate, Dotty looked disappointed, so Olivia added a dash of raspberry sauce in the middle.

"That there is a Jupiter pancake. Have you heard about Jupiter?" Olivia asked. Dotty shook her head, so Olivia continued. "It's the largest planet in our solar system. They call it a gas giant because it's made up entirely of gas."

Dotty's eyes widened as she cut a piece and put it in her mouth. Satisfied that Dotty was eating, Olivia washed up. When she turned back, the plate was empty, and Olivia stood there for a minute. Dotty still fiddled with her truck, so Olivia grasped at an idea. "Want to look at my books?"

Dotty's face lit up before she nodded, and Olivia led Dotty back to the hallway, truck in tow. The wonder returned, the young child's eyes darting from one part to the next. Olivia was about to give a tour when Dotty stopped in her tracks and pointed to the shelf. "That's my car."

"Is it? I found that on my front lawn a while ago, but I didn't know who it belonged to. Would you like it back?" Olivia asked. When Dotty nodded, Olivia reached out and lifted it off the shelf.

At the same time, she snagged a sheet of thin, glossy paper, which slowly fluttered to the floor, and a slimline framed photograph that fell with a soft thud. Dotty picked up the magazine paper while Olivia snatched the frame and checked it for cracks before carefully putting it back. It was a wedding photograph with the young bride and groom in front of a sign for MIT, marked '2021'.

Dotty studied the page in her hands and started reading aloud, her fluency catching on some of the longer words. As Olivia listened, her eyes filmed over with a small tear. The little one reminded her so much of herself, long ago. With a rough voice, she said, "Oh my, you're a good reader. Would you like to read some more for me?"

Dotty nodded, and when Olivia asked what they should read, the girl pointed at the sheet of magazine paper. Olivia's breath caught. "My husband loved gardening magazines, too. You can pick a few."

CHAPTER SIXTEEN

Magazine

Morning tea-time arrived too soon. Dotty had read the first magazine cover to cover, asking plenty of questions about the plants within. When Dotty paused at the difficult words, she looked to Olivia for help. She was about to reach for her second issue, but Olivia called for a break.

Dotty sat at the dining table as Olivia prepared tea and biscuits for herself, and a glass of milk for Dotty. The young girl asked Olivia whether she had seen the plants from the magazine.

"Actually, I do have some in my back garden. My husband planted them, but I look after them now. Although I'm not doing a very good job, I'm afraid..." Olivia arranged a tea tray, then carried the biscuits and drinks to the table.

Dotty took a biscuit and bit into it, chewing until her brow furrowed. "Where's Papa?"

Olivia's thoughts tangled her tongue. She still didn't know if Papa was Luke or James. Biting the bullet, she said, "He's not back from the hospital yet, dear."

"Oh… Susy was really sick. She went to the toilet and started crying," said Dotty, little shoulders slumping. Despite her worries, she took another bite of the biscuit before continuing. "Papa told me to call the ambulance."

Guilt bloomed in Olivia's chest, considering the possible cause, and reassured the girl. "We'll just wait for them here, dear. I'm not going anywhere."

Yesterday's antics still played on Olivia's mind, but she didn't want to scare Dotty with accusations. There might never be another chance to ask, though. Olivia waited for the little girl to finish chewing, then took the plunge. "Dotty, why did you decorate my lawn?"

Dotty stared at her biscuit, turning it around in her fingers. "Mmm… Me and Susy thought your lawn was so pretty, we wanted to decorate it so maybe we could play on it," she said, then stopped her fiddling to focus on Olivia. "Your front lawn is perfect for when your time comes. What's your back garden like?"

Dotty's innocence warmed Olivia's heart. She had to clear her throat. "It's very different from the front lawn. There are a variety of plants. It's like a temperate rainforest, because the back part of the house faces south and gets less sun than the lawn. It's where I feel like myself the most, very therapeutic."

Dotty nodded sagely, but her eyes had glazed over. Olivia probably lost her at the word 'temperate', but Dotty's face brightened. "Can I see it? Please?"

She cutely dragged out her plea until Olivia laughed. "Sure, though I must warn you, you have to be careful. It's a bit of a jungle out there."

CHAPTER SEVENTEEN

Garden

Once outside, they ambled along the path together. Remembering the passion Adam had for his garden, Olivia occasionally paused to stroke the soft petals of a flower or pinch off a dying stem. Fascinated, Dotty pointed out the plants she knew and recited their names, taking Olivia by surprise. Dotty had a sharp mind, so Olivia showed her how to care for them as they wound through the lush space.

"I like to do my gardening in the afternoon, once the plants have done their growing for the day," said Olivia. She explained how her husband had arranged the plants according to the sunlight as Dotty listened intently.

Someone called at the gate, and they peeked around the corner to find James waiting. Dotty ran to the gate and called out, "Daddy!"

"I thought I heard my girl… Hi, Olivia. Luke told me that Dotty was here. Thank you so much for looking after her," said James.

"It was a pleasure, dear. How is your other girl?" Olivia asked.

"We're still waiting for the test results, but she's recovering," said James, before smiling at Dotty. "Have you been good for Mrs Olivia?"

"Yes, Daddy. We've been gardening and reading and… pancakes," Dotty said, her words tumbling out in a rush.

"Oh really! You'll have to tell me all about it," James replied as Olivia unlatched her gate for Dotty to go out. Through the window, Dotty's truck and car sat on the table, having been forgotten by their owner, as their blanket of security was no longer needed.

CHAPTER EIGHTEEN

Arrangements

It was time to edge the lawn. Olivia found it had become overgrown again, and she regretted scaring off her little night-time helpers. She had brought the whipper snipper to the front and started it, when Luke appeared with her Tupperware box. He waved at her and stood there as he put the box down, waiting.

Olivia switched off the whipper snipper. "Hi, Luke."

"Hi, Olivia," Luke boomed across the short distance. "I just wanted to thank you for looking after Dotty. She hasn't stopped talking about all the things she learnt in your gardening magazine and what you showed her in your backyard."

Olivia squinted at the volume. "Oh, that's lovely, dear. She's a bright girl." She was silent, then blurted out.

"And your other daughter?"

"Susy's fine now. They think she had an allergic reaction to fruit," said Luke. Olivia's face flushed hot, but Luke seemed unaware as he swatted a fly buzzing around his face.

The petals of guilt exploded and whirled within her. Then she quickly decided. "I gave them some fruit during Halloween, toffee kiwi fruit…"

Luke stilled. "Ah… Yes, she's never had kiwi fruit before… I'm glad you told me, Olivia. It's an honest mistake." He fiddled at the low fence between them as smiled at her. "I brought some homemade biscuits for you and your Tupperware container. But you have your hands full, I see; I can put it by your door if you wish…"

Olivia put the whipper snipper down and held out her hands. "No, it's alright dear, I'll take it in," she insisted, as the Tupperware exchanged hands.

Luke remained standing there, tracing his fingers along the fence. "I wondered, if it's not too much trouble, could you please look after Dotty once a week? Just a few hours after school?"

Olivia hesitated. She'd been alone for so long, she had forgotten what it was like to have regular company. But, she admitted to herself, having Dotty over was a surprising comfort.

"I'll pay you, of course," Luke whispered, clutching the top of the fence and leaning over it.

Olivia made up her mind, the second time she had to in five minutes, and finally smiled back. "Yes, dear, I would love to."

They briefly discussed the details, and when Luke left, Olivia leaned against the fence, wistfully looking into the distance, a smile teasing her lips.

CHAPTER NINETEEN

Research

The next day, the doorbell rang, and Olivia opened her door. Dotty was standing there with her normal-sized school bag that appeared too large for her body.

"Come in, come in! How was school?"

"We learnt about Jupiter today. It's a gas giant like you said!" Dotty exclaimed as she walked through the door. She chattered happily as they walked into the kitchen. "My truck!"

Olivia could tell that Dotty had forgotten all about it. "Yes dear, it's been waiting for you since last time. Would you like to eat something? There's fruit on the table, do you like fruit?"

Dotty nodded and took an apple from the bowl on the table. She held it in both hands as she asked, "Olivia, are we doing gardening today?"

Olivia was pleased. "Yes, the days are getting longer, so we have plenty of time. Do you have any homework?"

Dotty shifted in her seat and fiddled with the truck. "Papa usually helps me with my homework after dinner."

Olivia was doubtful, but didn't say anything. "Okay then. Why don't we do some research before we go into the garden?"

"What's research?"

Olivia chose her words with care, conscious that her audience was only seven years old. "It means finding out things you didn't know before."

"Oh! Like at school!"

"Yes, something like that. Except you have a question, and you try to answer it yourself by reading."

"Oh." Dotty thought for a bit. "Can you ask the teacher?"

"I don't have a teacher, dear," Olivia said gently. "Come, I'll show you."

Olivia took Dotty to the gardening magazine rack in the

hallway. She took out a magazine with no pictures. "This is called an index. It's a way to look at all the different topics to help find the magazine you need. Is there anything you want to know more about, from what you read last time?"

"Umm..." Dotty thought. "What about basil?"

Olivia showed her the process of using the index, as Dotty watched intently. "Now, I'm concerned about leaf miners. Would you like to find some magazines for me?"

"Yes, I can do it!" Dotty said. She followed the procedure perfectly and found three magazines about the pest. Olivia looked on with pride.

"Thank you! Now, let's read about it."

Olivia guided Dotty to the front room. Dotty spread out on the couch while Olivia sat at her desk. With a notepad and pen in hand, Olivia jotted notes as Dotty read the articles aloud.

"Now that we have done some research, we know how to treat leaf miners on citrus. Let's go to the garden and apply what we've learnt," said Olivia.

Dotty's mouth circled to a small 'O'. "Is that why you do research?"

"Yes dear, usually there's a problem and we need to fix it. But sometimes, nobody has found the answer, which means someone has to do the experiments to find out." Olivia was no stranger to a research challenge.

"What's experiments?" Dotty asked, trying on the big word for size.

Olivia laughed and beckoned to her burgeoning kindred spirit. "Come on, I'll tell you outside in the garden."

CHAPTER TWENTY

December

For another few weeks, Dotty visited Olivia to help with her garden. School holidays were coming up, so the older woman wanted to know what was happening during the summer break. She had carefully planned what she would say to Luke when he picked up the girl that afternoon.

"I wish we had a pool," Dotty said.

"You can get an inflatable one," Olivia replied absentmindedly, as she clipped a stem off her kumquat shrub.

Dotty removed her gloves and dug the mini-dictionary from her pocket. It was on loan because Olivia didn't have all of the answers, and her new friend had so many questions. Olivia pre-empted the spelling question. "I-N-F-L-A-T-A-B-L-E."

"Capable of being filled with air," Dotty read out. She put the dictionary back into her pocket.

Olivia carefully snipped another stem and dropped it into the bucket. "You can probably buy one at Kmart."

Dotty wriggled her fingers back into the gardening gloves, then squatted to pull the weeds. Not the most exciting task for a youngster, but Dotty didn't seem to mind. She spied a snail eating Olivia's plants, and repositioned the motion sensitive camera they were using to make a stop-motion animation of the pest. Dotty was a good apprentice.

"Hello!" It was Luke at the gate.

"Papa!" Dotty cried. She ran to the gate, opened it, and hugged his legs. "Can we go to Kmart?"

"Sure," Luke looked perplexed. He turned to Olivia, outside voice on, as usual. "How was everything?"

"All good, dear. Actually, I have something I want to talk to you about."

"Oh? Me too, but you first," Luke replied.

"Well, I was wondering if Dotty would like to come

over during the school holidays?"

"Oh, that's a relief. I wanted to ask the same question, but I didn't want to be rude." They both laughed and Luke smiled at her. "I would be happy if Dotty kept coming here regularly. James and I have noticed how much Dotty's come out of her shell since she met you. Usually she just follows what Susy does when they're at home together."

Olivia simply smiled in return, unable to confess how much she enjoyed the company.

CHAPTER TWENTY-ONE

Cats

"It's going to be a hot one today," Olivia thought, remembering last night's weather forecast. She stretched her body, joints clicking through the motions, and rose to start the day. It was still dark outside, but she headed to the kitchen to prepare her breakfast. As she passed the front room, she glanced at her video feed to see the cat on her lawn about to do the deed.

She turned into the front room and opened the window, loudly whispering, "Shoo! Shoo!" at the cat. The cat turned towards her lazily, finished its business slowly, and sauntered away. Olivia still hadn't figured out the frustrating cat's movements (in both senses of the word). Whilst the motion detectors picked it up, the microphones did not. She could not figure out how to get rid of it. It was one sneaky kitty.

A few hours later, Dotty arrived at her door. They

chatted about the garden, but the conversation quickly turned towards the cat on her front lawn, as it often did. Unlike the other times they talked, Dotty sat up straight, like a lightbulb switched on above her head.

"Why don't you adopt it!" she cried.

Frowning, Olivia followed her new routine and set a snack in front of Dotty. "I don't know anything about cats."

"We could research it, like the garden…"

Olivia was uncertain. At this late stage of her life, taking on a creature who'd depend on her seemed unwise. What would happen after she passed away? However, the street cat had survived on its own this whole time.

"Okay, we can research, but no promises I'll adopt it." There was a full stop in her tone.

CHAPTER TWENTY-TWO

Books

The next day, the library delivered cat care books to Olivia's home. The two were in the garden, weeding, and Dotty jumped up. Hopping from foot to foot, the girl squealed. "Olivia! They're here!"

"Okay, dear, go get them and read one to me."

Dotty fetched the book bag from the door and read out the titles. 'Owning a Cat', 'Raising Puss', and 'Kittens: The First 30 Days' were just some.

Olivia didn't look up from her weeding. "Any one of them will do."

Dotty chose the one with the cutest image of a fuzzball on the cover and started reading. An hour later, she reached the end, excited.

"Olivia, what if we left it some food on the lawn? Maybe it will stop pooping there because it eats there?"

Olivia hesitated. It seemed counterintuitive to reward the cat's bad behaviour, but the general logic made sense from what Dotty had just read. "Hmm, it's worth a try. I'll put some food out this evening."

Olivia continued gardening while Dotty read out another book to her.

CHAPTER TWENTY-THREE

Partay

Christmas morning, and Olivia's house was the same as ever—not a decoration to be seen. Olivia had resisted the holiday tradition, despite Dotty's understandable excitement and wheedling. She'd almost given in, wanting to please the girl.

"But it was just another day," Olivia thought as her bones warmed up with exercise. She headed to the kitchen for breakfast, and although it was still early, she heard animated chatter coming from next door. Olivia assumed the kids were opening their presents.

She thought about her own children, with their children and grandchildren, probably having a similar situation play out in their own homes far away. She didn't speak to them much anymore, they had their own lives to live. The squeals gradually made their way outside and to the front. Then everything became quiet. Eerily quiet.

Olivia opened her front window to look outside. It was Dotty and her sister Susy, in their pyjamas, stringing tinsel through her bushes and along the fence. They also had what looked like a deflated inflatable pool.

"Get off my lawn!" Olivia called out in a mock angry tone, and Dotty's mischievous giggle floated back.

"We're bringing Christmas to you, Mrs. Olivia!" Dotty cried. After Susy finished her decorating, she crouched down to pet the cat. With a regularly full belly, the animal quite liked people now.

Olivia closed the window and hustled to her bedroom. A few minutes later, she came out, flaunting a dated but glamorous swimming costume. She grabbed a bottle of lemon squash and disposable cups, then dashed outside as fast as she could.

"I might as well join the party on my own lawn!" She looked around for somewhere to sit. "Dotty, could you please get the chairs in my back garden?"

Dotty nodded and flew through the gate to the back, leaving Susy behind. There was an awkward silence while they waited for her to return. "Dotty has told me all about you... I see you've made friends with the cat."

Susy kept stroking the black fur. "Me and Dotty were wondering what his name is."

"Oh, is it a boy cat?"

"Yes, I looked."

Olivia hummed. "I'm not sure what his name is. What do you think?"

"He kind of feels like a Rodrigo..." Susy scratched the cat under his chin, as the cat turned his head closer to Susy's hand for a better angle.

Dotty came back with two stools. "I can't lift the deck chair, Olivia."

"Oh, that isn't meant to be moved, dear. I'll fetch the banana lounge from the garage. You two blow up the pool with the pump and fill it up with water. Here's a cool drink."

Olivia set up the banana lounge next to the inflated pool, and the girls started filling it using the hose. Luke came out of their house.

"No wonder it's been so quiet in the house! You two have been out here," said Luke, laughing heartily. "Breakfast is ready, and we have Christmas pancakes."

"Yay!" the two girls said in unison as they ran into their

house.

"Sorry about this, Olivia. I just turned my back for a second and they were gone. I can take the decorations off your lawn..."

"No, it's alright, dear. A lawn is alive to be enjoyed." Olivia surprised herself by saying that. She'd been so used to maintaining the lawn for the sake of the lawn, she'd forgotten its purpose. "Come join me later, if you wish. I look rather ridiculous in my swimmers on my front lawn all by myself."

Luke smiled. "Okay. If you like, we can set up the barbeque in the driveway and eat lunch together."

CHAPTER TWENTY-FOUR

Last

The pool party wouldn't be forgotten too soon. Various neighbours on the street walked past, and some joined them for a short while. As Olivia, Luke, and James cleared the plates, Dotty and Susy paddled in the inflatable pool, deep in discussion about something. Rodrigo kept far away from the splashing water.

"Kids, are you coming in? Your fingers will be like prunes," said Luke, as he brought the plates in.

"But it's so hot, Papa!" Susy shouted back, loud like Luke.

"I'm going in now," Dotty said, jumping from the pool to run back to her house. Susy hung around for a bit, but without her playmate, she slowly followed. James lingered on the lawn with Olivia.

"They are charming girls," said Olivia.

James grinned with pride. "Yes, they're a handful, but no regrets."

"This was an unexpected Christmas celebration for me, so thank you."

"You can thank Luke for not paying attention."

"Thank you, Luke!" Olivia cried with outstretched arms as Luke came out of the house.

"For what?" Luke asked, and the others laughed. He scanned the yard. "Well, if there's nothing else, I'll head back in. Who knows what the girls will do next?"

"Thank you for the day, I couldn't have asked for anything better," said Olivia. She left the chairs and the pool on her lawn, and shuffled inside.

A few hours later, Olivia started her bedtime routine. First, she took a shower, then put on her nightclothes, before checking her house was locked. Olivia retired to her room and lay in bed, wondering if she needed to change anything in her day, and she couldn't find a thing. Content, she closed her eyes in the darkness for the last time.

CHAPTER TWENTY-FIVE

March

Dotty purposefully walked to the local library with Susy after school. Since Olivia passed away, this was where she preferred to be, surrounded by books like in Olivia's hallway. She leisurely browsed for a couple of hours, choosing from the titles and bringing them home in her book bag.

When she reached her house, she noticed a man in a grey suit. He stood still on Olivia's lawn, looking off into the distance. Olivia wouldn't like that. "Excuse me, sir, could you please get off the lawn?"

Surprised, he turned his head towards her. "Are you Dotty?"

"I'm not allowed to talk to strangers!" Dotty shouted, as she ran into her house, slammed the front door, and put her weight on it.

Before long, there was a knock on the door, and Papa shifted Dotty to answer it. "Yes?"

"I'm Hugh, one of Olivia's sons. I believe you are Luke or James?" he said, with an air of corporate confidence.

"That's right, I'm Luke."

"Hi, nice to meet you. I'm here to clear out Mum's house before it's sold. She's mentioned you and Dotty in her instructions a few times." Hugh pulled out some photographs and a small box from his pocket. "We found these amongst Mum's things and thought you might like them."

Hugh presented the photos to Papa, who cycled through them. Papa absentmindedly handed over the photos and a small box to Dotty while he continued to talk to Hugh. "Ah yes. Dotty, come look at these, it's from Mrs. Olivia."

Dotty stared at the first photo of herself reading a gardening magazine. She flipped to the next one to find a crooked photo that Dotty took of Olivia smelling a flower. Dotty touched the image of Olivia's face, a tear falling down her cheek. She shuffled through the photos, ignoring the two men speaking in the doorway.

Dotty slowly walked into the living room, eyes down.

Papa shut the door before following Dotty. He stretched out his arms for a big hug. "Dotty, come here."

"I don't know if you heard any of that, but Mrs. Olivia wanted you to have a few things. Mainly she wanted you to have your pick of the books on her shelves. But you can't take all of them because we don't have room." He pressed a kiss to her forehead. "I think it was Mrs. Olivia's way of saying goodbye to you."

Dotty nodded, but focussed on the photos in her hands, unable to say anything. Papa gently stroked her hair. "You can come home straight after school tomorrow, and I'll take you."

CHAPTER TWENTY-SIX

Goodbye

As the sun began to set, Dotty and Susy snuck out of their window. In Dotty's hand was Olivia's gift to her, a small drone, and her toy car, the one she accidentally left on Olivia's lawn all those months ago. They walked to the middle of her lawn.

"Bye, Mrs. Olivia," Dotty whispered and had started to crouch when a shadow streaked past. It was Rodrigo hunting for his evening meal.

"What do you think, should we feed Rodrigo again? I kinda want a cat," Susy said.

Dotty finished putting her toy car down into the overgrown grass, her shrine to Olivia complete. She threw her drone into the air, where it hovered, made a sound of a camera shutter, then slowly landed on her outstretched palm. "Whatever will keep him off the lawn."

THE END